E
Jac

CHICKEN TEN THOUSAND

By Jacqueline Jackson

For my father—
a proven sire
who'd rather bet on a yard egg

CHICKEN TEN THOUSAND

by JACQUELINE JACKSON

illustrated by BARBARA MORROW

LITTLE, BROWN AND COMPANY   BOSTON   TORONTO

Published simultaneously in Canada
by Little, Brown & Company (Canada) Limited

PRINTED IN THE UNITED STATES OF AMERICA

Row on row
tray above tray
were ten thousand look-alike eggs
in a warm egg-hatcher.
The hatcher was more than hen-cosy
for it never scratched after a burrowing bug
and let the eggs cool.
It was more than hen-careful
for it never failed to turn
each egg
exactly twice a day.

5

No need for hens—
except to lay ten thousand
look-alike
eggs.

6

Secret within the shells
ten thousand pulsing hearts sent out
threads of red
that veined the yellow yokes.
Secret grew the transparent eyes
the curled claws
the damp and clinging down.

Twenty-one days from yoke to chick
and the trays were filled
with tapping and cracking.
Little Ten Thousand stood
wobble-legged
beside her shattered shell
peeping glad cheeps
for joy of life.

From the hatcher to the bander
went the chicks
for each to get a
numbered metal anklet

and from the bander to the brooder
which had sawdust on the floor
and chick feed in a trough
and water in a never-empty pan
while close overhead a glowing globe
poured down endless beams of warmth.

9

Little Ten Thousand along with
nine thousand nine hundred ninety-nine
other chicks
peeped and pecked and drank
and ran around
and her neck grew long
and feather tips
crowded out her tawny fuzz

and with all the other gangly chickens
she went
from brooder to the growing pen
and grew into a pullet
and was moved
another time

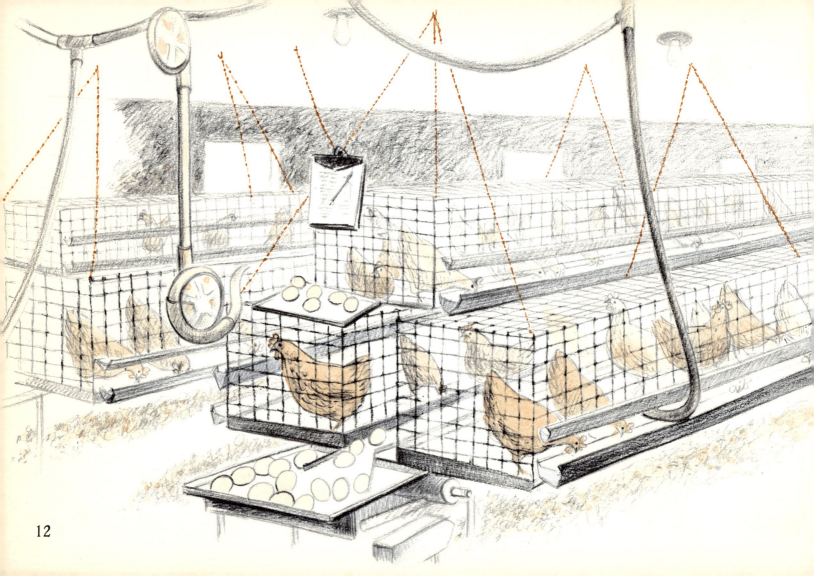

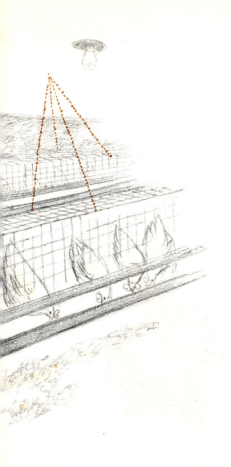

to a wire cage just big enough
to hold one hen
and row on row
above and below
in other cages other hens
poked out their heads
to peck the feed
and gurgle down the water.
And every now and then
came instant dark
for exactly six hours.

After a bit
Little Ten Thousand
felt a strangeness within
a swelling and stirring
as if she were
about to *lay* something
and then
she *did* lay something
and she cackled a cut-cut-cut-
caDAWcut of joy and pulled in her head
but nothing was there
nothing
except the hole in the mesh
of the cage floor.

14

Time went by and
the feeling came again.
Once more
Little Ten Thousand's heart quickened
and this time
after she had laid something
she didn't pause to cackle.
With all hen-speed she cocked her head
but there was nothing
nothing.

A sadness filled
Little Ten Thousand's chicken heart.
She had not been quick enough to see
whatever it was
slip through the wires
roll gently down a slope
to the collection area

where it was washed and
checked and weighed and where
a vacuum gripper placed it
and eleven others of its kind
inside a cardboard carton
behind a hundred other cartons
on an endless moving belt.

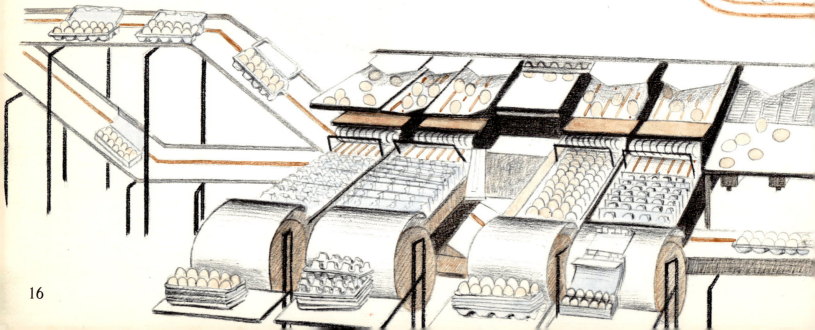

Little Ten Thousand grew broody.
She didn't peck
she didn't drink
a dullness filmed her eyes
and her crimson wattles faded.

She no longer bothered to look
and the mysterious
promising feeling
came less and less and finally
not at all.

"So you're comfortable," clucked a neighbor.
"So why worry?"

"Life is a husk," sighed Little Ten Thousand
and her chicken heart
was bitter.

One day she was taken from her cage
and jammed into a crate
full of tough and stringy fowl
too old to lay
good only for market
and chicken soup.
The crate was slung up
on a load of crates
and the truck rumbled away.

But on a curve
the topmost crate slid off.
Chickens squawked
feathers flew
the crate lit and split
and Little Ten Thousand squeezed out.
She scuttled into a ditch
while the truck backed up
and while the crate was tied
more firmly.
Then the truck roared away
and all was quiet.

Little Ten Thousand
poked out her head.
What was this green sawdust
that felt so cool
and smelled so sweet?
What was this brown floor
so rough and scratchy under claw
with tasty tidbits scurrying around?

Purling with pleasure
Little Ten Thousand scratched and pecked
until she came to what must be
the largest water pan in all the world.
She took a swallow and as the water
trickled down her gullet
she saw above   only brighter
a gold ball like the brooder globe   and warmer
when she was but a chick   and more dazzling.

21

The ball sank low
turned red
and slipped from sight.
Little Ten Thousand had never known
day to fade
so gradually

but she tucked her head under her wing
and slept.

"Cock-a-doodle—
dooooooooooooooooooooo!"

Across the water pan
the great globe was just rising
and before her stood the
most splendid creature
she had ever seen.

"Who are you?" asked Little Ten Thousand.

"An adventurer
a wanderer
and the boldest rooster in Vickland Township,"
said the proud plumed stranger
with a toss of his scarlet comb.
"I have chicks beyond number
and four hundred ninety-nine wives
at last count.
You may be the five hundredth
if you like
but I must be off before long."

25

When the rooster had gone
Little Ten Thousand was somewhat lonely
but still she had
the soft green sawdust
and the brown floor
full of crawling chicken feed
and the huge rippling water pan
and the warm bulb
that wandered slowly across the blue ceiling.

Then one day
the long-dead laying feeling
began to stir. "Oh, no,"
sighed Little Ten Thousand.
"I thought I had left behind forever
that deceiving feeling
that betraying feeling
that bitter disappointment after promise!"

But she found herself scratching
a hollow in the brown floor
and turning round and round
and settling down.

And *this* time
after she thought she'd
laid something
she didn't need to look
for she could feel it
hard and smooth beneath her feathers
but look she did
at the tan something lying in the dust
and "Cut-cut-cut-caDAWcut!"
she cackled for joy.

Every day she laid
another
until there wasn't room
for any more
and then she settled down on them.

28

She warmed them all the time
except when she went
for a brisk scratch to find
breakfast
or for a quick gurgle
from the giant pan.
She turned them every day
except when she forgot
or turned one twice
and another not at all.

and Little Ten Thousand
peeked beneath
her fluffed-out bosom
to see beside a shattered shell
a damp and downy chick.
Another shell began to crack
and yet another

And after many days
there came a tapping and a cracking

till by the time the golden globe
was flooding the water pan
with liquid fire
ten wobble-legged chicks
came scrambling and falling
when Little Ten Thousand
clucked them home to rest.

With sleepy cheeps they clustered
underneath her spreading feathers
and Little Ten Thousand
in her chicken heart
was content.